♥ p u p p y & m e ♥

Breakfast Time

Carol Stream Public Library
Carol Stream, Illinois 60188

Withdrawn

P9-DXT-006

by Julia Noonan

Cartwheel
·B·O·O·K·S·®

SCHOLASTIC INC.

New York   Toronto   London   Auckland   Sydney   Mexico City   New Delhi   Hong Kong

Here's my bib, and
   here's my spoon.
Food is coming
   very soon!
Puppy barks a
   breakfast tune.

We both sing for breakfast.

Mommy! Look what
we can do!
I use toast for
peek-a-boo.
Then I eat it.
Pup does, too.

Crunchy, munchy breakfast.

Now I drop my
favorite cup!
Juice spills on the
floor near Pup.
I watch Puppy
lick it up!

Puppy cleans at breakfast.

I make corn flakes
fall like snow.
Puppy watches
from below.
Catches every one
I throw!

Puppy's fast at breakfast.

Puppy dances!
  Then he begs.
Then he helps me
  eat my eggs.
He licks yogurt
  off my legs.

Tickle-time at breakfast.

Mommy takes my
bowl and cup.
Giant washcloth
cleans us up.
I am full, and
so is Pup!

Tummies full of breakfast.

New clothes come when
food is done.
Time for Pup and
me to run!
Find a morning
full of fun.

Now that we've had breakfast.

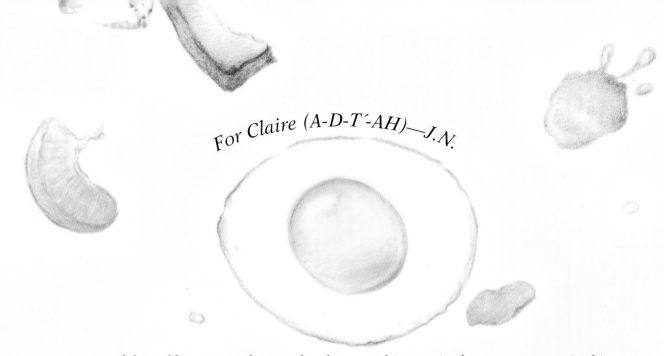

For Claire (A-D-T´-AH)—J.N.

No part of this publication may be reproduced, or stored in a retrieval system, or transmitted in any form or by any means, electronic, mechanical, photocopying, recording, or otherwise, without written permission of the publisher. For information regarding permission, write to Scholastic Inc., Attention: Permissions Department, 555 Broadway, New York, NY 10012.

ISBN 0-439-11490-X

Copyright © 2000 by Julia Noonan.
All rights reserved. Published by Scholastic Inc.
SCHOLASTIC, CARTWHEEL BOOKS and associated logos are trademarks and/or registered trademarks of Scholastic Inc.

12 11 10 9 8 7 6 5 4 3 2 1   0/0 01 02 03 04 05

Printed in Malaysia   46
First printing, June 2000